For Edie - M.R. x

To G.C. with love - R.B. x

Farshore

First published in Great Britain 2021 by Farshore
An imprint of HarperCollins*Publishers*
1 London Bridge Street, London SE1 9GF
www.farshorebooks.com

HarperCollins*Publishers*
1st Floor, Watermarque Building, Ringsend Road
Dublin 4, Ireland

Text copyright © Michelle Robinson 2021
Illustrations copyright © Rosalind Beardshaw 2021

Michelle Robinson and Rosalind Beardshaw have asserted their moral rights.

ISBN 978 1 4052 9567 3
Printed in Italy.
1

A CIP catalogue record for this title is available from the British Library.

1, 2, 3, DO THE SHARK

Michelle Robinson & Rosalind Beardshaw

Farshore

Deep beneath the waves, in the middle of the ocean,

A great big storm was whipping all the seaweed into motion.

Bess's fishy friends were just as **frightened** as can be. So she flipped her tail and told them,

"Don't be scared, just copy me . . .

"Pretend to be a shark," she said.
"They **never** run and hide.

Just **clap** your hands like **mighty jaws**,
then open them out wide.

1, 2, 3,

do the **clapping** shark with me!

Everybody **boogie** at the bottom of the sea."

Her friends **all** tried their best.

"But, Bess,
the ocean's **deep**
and **dark!**"

"There's nothing to be scared of!
Copy me and **do the shark!**

"Hands up **high**, just like a fin.
Pretend you're **big** and **tough**.

Wave your pointy fin, then **swish** your tail
and **strut** your stuff!

1, 2, 3, do the **waving** shark with me!

Everybody **boogie** at the bottom of the sea."

"Let's head a little deeper," Bess said.
"Time to take a dive.

Arms out straight like arrows,
Hold your breath and count to **five!**

1, 2, 3,
do the diving shark with me!

4, 5,
dive to the bottom of the sea!"

The little turtle said, "Look out!
There's something in that cave."

"Nothing frightens sharks!" said Bess.
Her friends weren't quite so brave . . .

"SHARK!" cried Crab.

"Uh-oh!" said Bess. "Let's hide inside this wreck."

She **hugged** her buddies tightly
as they hid below the deck.

"1, 2, 3,
do the **silent** shark with me!

Hush! Don't
make a sound!
We sharks are
quiet as can be."

The real shark clapped
its **giant jaws!**

It **waved** its **pointy fin**.

It **dived** into their hiding place –
and said . . .

"CAN I JOIN IN?

I've been **so lonely** on my own –
I'd love to have some **fun.**"

"Just copy us," Bess told him.
"And, please, don't eat anyone!"

The starfish did
a **star jump**

and the dab fish
did a **dab**.

The shark
was turning
cartwheels
with the turtle
and the crab.

The storm was long forgotten.
They were **partying** in style!

Until the shark's mouth opened **wide** . . .

Into a great white **smile**.

1, 2, 3,

Come on . . . do the shark with me!

And everybody **boogied** at the bottom of the sea.

The little crab was yawning.
Soon the others started too.
Bess smiled and whispered softly,
"There's just **one more**
move to do.

Give your fins a nice **big stretch**.

Now wrap them round you **tight**.

Everybody **snuggle** down.

1, 2, 3...

"Sleep tight!"